This Book Belongs to:

Mickey's Young Readers Library

VOLUME
17
Donald and the Frog

STORY BY MARY PACKARD

Activities by Thoburn Educational Enterprises, Inc.

A BANTAM BOOK
NEW YORK · TORONTO · LONDON · SYDNEY · AUCKLAND

Donald and the Frog A Bantam Book/September 1990. All rights reserved. © 1990 The Walt Disney Company. Developed by
The Walt Disney Company in conjunction with Nancy Hall, Inc. This book may not be reproduced or transmitted in any form or by any means.
ISBN 0–553–05632–8
Published simultaneously in the United States and Canada. Bantam Books are published by Bantam Doubleday Dell Publishing Group,
Inc. Its trademark, consisting of the words "Bantam Books" and the portrayal of a rooster, is Registered in U.S. Patent
and Trademark Office and in other countries. Marca Registrada. Bantam Books 666 Fifth Avenue, New York, New York 10103.
Printed in the United States of America
0 9 8 7 6 5 4 3 2 1
A Walt Disney BOOK FOR YOUNG READERS

One sunny day Donald woke up feeling great.
"What a perfect day for the Junior Woodchuck
picnic!" he said with a smile.

Donald was a den uncle. He had entered his
Junior Woodchucks in all the contests that were
planned for the day. He had been training them for
nine weeks.

He kicked off the covers and jumped out of bed.
He touched his toes ten times, and he did eight
sit-ups. Then he did six push-ups.

"I've got to be in shape for the den-uncle boat
race," he said to himself. "Something tells me I'm
going to win it this time!"

When Donald arrived at the park, the
Woodchucks were already there. Grandma Duck
was there, too. Beside her was a big basket of food.
"Hi, Uncle Donald!" cried Huey, Dewey, and
Louie.

"Hi, boys," replied Donald. "I see you're already warming up for the contests. I hope you made plenty of pies this year, Grandma," he added. "After we win all seven contests, we'll be mighty hungry."

"Time for the relay race!" somebody shouted.
Donald's team lined up, one behind the other.
Soon they heard the starting whistle. The race
began! Dewey was the first to run and quickly took
the lead.

"Way to go, Dewey!" his teammates cheered.
Huey's turn was second, and Louie's was third.

Before they knew it, Louie had crossed the
finish line.

"We won!" cried Donald.

The three Junior Woodchucks stood tall as he
pinned blue ribbons to their shirts.

"You did a great job!" Donald said happily. "I'm
proud of you!"

Before long, it was time for the tug of war.

"Uh-oh!" groaned Louie, when he saw the other team. "They're very big!"

"Just do your best," said Donald. "We promised we would play. And a promise is a promise."

Donald cheered with all his might. But it didn't
do any good.

Louie pulled. Huey tugged. Dewey yanked. They
all dug in their feet and leaned back. But no matter
how hard they tried, they couldn't hold their places.
The tug of war was over in no time. The other team
had won.

"Hey, boys," said Donald. "Don't look so unhappy. You can't win them all."

"Is there anything we could have done differently?" asked Huey.

"Sure," answered Louie. "We could have grown about two feet and gained a hundred pounds each!"

"I like you just the way you are," said Donald. "And I'm proud of you, too. You are good sports. You tried your best, and that's all that really matters."

Before long, it was time for the rowing race.
All the den uncles got into their boats.
Soon the whistle sounded, and the five rowers
were off. Donald's Junior Woodchucks cheered and
cheered:
"One, two, three, four
Who will be the first to shore?
Uncle Donald! Uncle Donald! Uncle Donald!"

Donald rowed harder than he had ever rowed before. When he looked up, he saw that he was in the lead.

"Boy-oh-boy-oh-boy!" he cried. "I'm going to win this race for sure! That trophy sure will look good over the fireplace! Or maybe I'll put it in my bedroom. That way I'll see it first thing every morning!"

Donald stopped rowing. He stood up in the boat. He wanted to see just how far ahead he really was. But before he sat down again, Donald heard a splash. He turned around just in time to see his oar floating away.

"Oh, no!" he cried. Donald grabbed the other oar and paddled as hard as he could. But he just kept spinning around in circles.

Donald was getting dizzy from all that spinning.
He closed his eyes. When he opened them again, he
saw a big bullfrog sitting on a lily pad. The lily pad
was very close to his lost oar.

The frog followed as the Junior Woodchucks carried Donald over to receive his trophy. A big crowd was waiting for them. They cheered as Donald held up the first prize.

"Just a little farther to go," Donald thought.
Sure enough—just a few more strokes brought
Donald sailing across the finish line.
"You won, Uncle Donald!" cried Louie.
"Hurray!" the others cheered.
"The trophy is mine!" cried Donald.

The frog cleared his throat. "Excuse me, but what about your promise?" he asked.
Donald didn't answer.
The frog was getting angry.

Donald tried to ignore the frog who was
standing right beside him. The frog tugged at
Donald's foot. But Donald pretended not to feel it.

"Oh great—a talking frog!" cried Donald. "Maybe you can help me. Do you think you could push that little oar over to my boat?" asked Donald.

"That's a pretty big oar, if you ask me," said the frog. "I could do it, but it would not be easy."

"I see you have a problem," said the frog.
Donald blinked his eyes. Then he shook his head. He didn't believe he had just heard the frog speak.
"The sun must be stronger than I thought," he said.
The frog spoke again. "I said, I see you've lost your oar!"

When they were alone, Donald said, "I'm the one who won the trophy, not you!"

"You never would have won that trophy without my help," replied the frog. "Besides, a promise is a promise!" he declared.

"I want my trophy, and I want it now!" croaked the frog.

Donald quickly excused himself. Then he led the frog away.

It didn't take Donald long to catch up with the others. In fact, it wasn't long before he was way ahead of them again. Donald could see the finish line. And he could hear his Woodchucks cheering him on.

"It's a deal," smiled the frog. And with that he hopped from lily pad to lily pad. He pushed that oar with all his might. The frog huffed and puffed. One final push, and Donald could reach the oar.

The frog flopped down on the lily pad. He gave a big sigh. "See you later," he panted. But Donald didn't hear him. He was back in the race!

"But I'm in a race," Donald explained quickly.
"Without that oar, I can't win! Please push it over
here," he begged. "I'll be so grateful!"
"How grateful?" asked the frog.

Donald could see that the other boats were catching up.

"I'll give you anything," Donald promised.

"What could you give me to make me want to help you?" asked the clever frog.

"Anything you want! You can have my trophy!" said Donald. "It's a little golden rowboat—just your size!"

"I'll give you my favorite pen, instead," Donald offered lamely.

"I don't want your pen," replied the frog firmly. "Now pay up!"

Donald sadly placed the trophy in the water, and the frog rowed away.

Donald muttered to himself as he walked away from the lake. His Junior Woodchucks ran after him.

"What were you doing with that frog?" asked Louie.

"Could we see your trophy?" asked Huey.

"I have something to tell you," said Donald. "I dropped my oar in the lake during the race. That frog helped me get it back, and I promised him my trophy. So I gave it to him."

"You gave him your trophy?" asked Louie.

"Yes," answered Donald. "But I guess I don't mind. After all, a promise is a promise." But Donald looked unhappy.

Donald stared out over the lake. He was thinking about his lost trophy. He looked very sad.

"I don't care what he says," declared Dewey. "I think Uncle Donald wishes that he still had his trophy. He hasn't even eaten one piece of Grandma's pie yet!"

"Why don't we make him a special award?" suggested Louie.

"Great idea!" agreed the other Woodchucks. "That should cheer him up." They quickly set to work. And when they were finished, they rounded up everybody again.

"Will Uncle Donald please step up," called Huey.
"What's this all about?" asked Donald.
"We want to give you the 'Best Sport' award for keeping your promise, and for giving your wonderful trophy to the frog," announced Huey. Then he handed Donald the award they had made him. It was a wooden oar on which they had carved the words "Best Sport."

"Thanks, fellas!" said Donald. "It looks like this is my lucky day after all. Has anybody seen Grandma? I think I'm ready to have some of that pie now!"

Think About It

What Happened When?

Look at the pictures below. Point to them in the order in which they happened in the story.

After your child does the activities in this book, refer to the *Young Readers Guide* for the answers to these activities and for additional games, activities, and ideas.

Be A Good Sport

1. What did Donald tell Huey, Dewey, and Louie when they lost the tug-of-war contest?

2. What did Donald promise the frog in return for his help?

3. Was Donald a good sport at first when the frog came to collect the trophy?

4. Do you think Donald deserved the "Best Sport" award after all? Explain why.

Fun With Words

Number Match

Help Donald match the numerals on these ribbons to their proper number words.

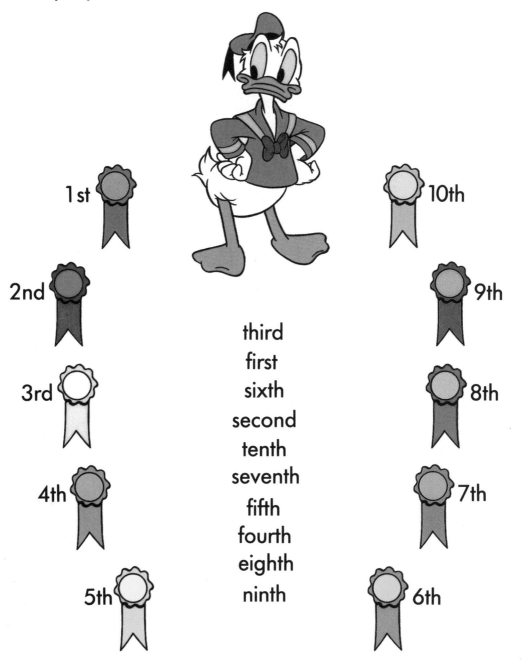

1st

10th

2nd

9th

third
first
sixth
second
tenth
seventh
fifth
fourth
eighth
ninth

3rd

8th

4th

7th

5th

6th

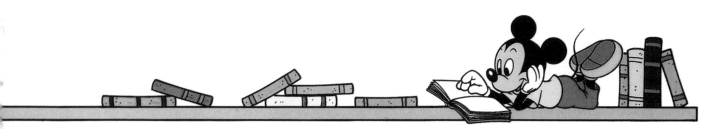

Words of Sportsmanship

See how many words you can make with the letters in the word SPORTSMANSHIP.